"Duz!" I called.

Duz didn't come.

"Maybe that name doesn't work anymore," Pamela said. "Genghis!" she called.

Duz didn't come.

I was getting a bad feeling.

I felt clammy and shivery.

I had guarded Duz, I had watched over him, and now . . .

What I had been afraid of . . . had it happened?

First Stepping Stone Books you will enjoy:

By David A. Adler
(The Houdini Club Magic Mystery series)
Onion Sundaes

By Mary Pope Osborne
(The Magic Tree House series)
Dinosaurs Before Dark (#1)
The Knight at Dawn (#2)
Mummies in the Morning (#3)
Pirates Past Noon (#4)

By Barbara Park
Junie B. Jones and the Stupid Smelly Bus
Junie B. Jones and a Little Monkey Business
Junie B. Jones and Her Big Fat Mouth
Junie B. Jones and Some Sneaky Peeky Spying

By Louis Sachar
Marvin Redpost: Kidnapped at Birth?
Marvin Redpost: Why Pick on Me?
Marvin Redpost: Is He a Girl?
Marvin Redpost: Alone in His Teacher's House

By Marjorie Weinman Sharmat
The Great Genghis Khan Look-Alike Contest
Genghis Khan: A Dog Star Is Born

GENGHIS KHAN
A Dog STAR IS BORN

by Marjorie Weinman Sharmat

illustrated by Mitchell Rigie

A FIRST STEPPING STONE BOOK
Random House New York

For my dog, Dudley,
who ... attention, all talent scouts! ... can breathe,
sit, stand, and needs a job. Did I mention that he's
also a Rhodes scholar?   *M. W. S.*

To Max
Thanks for keeping me company up in the studio all
those wintry days and nights.   *M. R.*

Text copyright © 1994 by Marjorie Weinman Sharmat
Illustrations copyright © 1994 by Mitchell Rigie
All rights reserved under International and Pan-American
Copyright Conventions. Published in the United States by
Random House, Inc., New York, and simultaneously in Canada
by Random House of Canada Limited, Toronto.

Library of Congress Cataloging-in-Publication Data
Sharmat, Marjorie Weinman. Genghis Khan: a dog star is born / by
Marjorie Weinman Sharmat ; illustrated by Mitchell Rigie.
   p. cm. "A First stepping stone book."
Sequel to: The great Genghis Khan look-alike contest.
SUMMARY: Fred Shedd and his parents accompany their dog Duz to
Hollywood, where his new career as a movie star is almost ended
before it begins when Duz is kidnapped.
ISBN 0-679-85406-1 (pbk.) — ISBN 0-679-95406-6 (lib. bdg.)
[1. Dogs—Fiction. 2. Motion pictures—Production and direction—Fiction.
3. Kidnapping—Fiction.] I. Rigie, Mitchell, ill. II. Title.
PZ7.S5299Gbf 1994 [Fic]—dc20 93-46233

Manufactured in the United States of America 10 9 8 7 6 5 4 3 2

OSCAR and ACADEMY AWARDS are registered trademarks of the Academy of
Motion Picture Arts and Sciences. This book is neither authorized nor
endorsed by the Academy of Motion Picture Arts and Sciences.

GENGHIS KHAN

A $\overset{Dog}{\wedge}$ STAR IS BORN

My dog is the most famous dog in the world.

He's a movie star.

I kept thinking about that on the plane trip to Hollywood. I was in first class. With my mother and father. And my dog, of course.

The flight attendant asked my dog for his autograph. Or a piece of fluff from his fur. Anything to prove she had actually met him.

He raised an ear. He could do this even before he became famous.

Actually, he used to be a plain dog. A

stray. One day he found me. Or I found him. I'm not sure who did the finding.

Anyway, what I couldn't find was his real owner. I tried hard. No luck.

So I kept the dog. I named him Duz. Because when people saw him, they always asked, "*Does* he bite?" Duz is really nice. But he looks very mean. I mean VERY.

I decided that he looked just like Genghis Khan, the movie-star dog. So I entered him in THE GREAT GENGHIS KHAN LOOK-ALIKE CONTEST.

Duz won. The old Genghis retired to a farm.

This is how my stray dog became Genghis Khan, the internationally famous movie star.

Even though he had never been in a movie!

As I looked out the plane window, I

thought about that. It was like getting an A in a test you haven't taken yet.

Duz was supposed to be Genghis for a year. A whole year in Hollywood! For Duz, my mother and father, and me, Fred Shedd.

The only bad thing about leaving home was saying good-bye to my best friend, Pamela Brinkman. She saw us off at the airport. She said, "I'll visit you. I promise."

She hugged Duz. "See you in the movies, famous dog."

Duz raised an ear and wagged his tail. He didn't know what it meant to be famous.

Yet.

2

A cheering crowd was waiting at the Los Angeles airport. WELCOME, GENGHIS KHAN signs were everywhere.

Duz sniffed madly. He was so excited. All these new people to sniff!

Reporters were shouting questions.

"WHAT IS GENGHIS'S FAVORITE FOOD?"

"WHAT ADVICE DOES GENGHIS HAVE FOR OTHER DOGS WHO WANT TO BE MOVIE STARS?"

"IS THIS A DOGGONE GOOD CAREER?"

"WHAT ARE GENGHIS'S BEAUTY SECRETS?"

"This is thrilling!" my mother said. "Our dog is famous. That makes us famous too. Doesn't it?"

Someone tugged at my sleeve. It was a big man in a chauffeur's uniform.

"My name is Fritz," he said. "I have a limo for you."

Fritz cleared the way through the crowd.

"Welcome to show biz," he said.

The limo was fantastic! The longest car I had ever seen. And it was silver.

Fritz held the door open for Duz. Duz wagged his tail, jumped in, and sniffed the leather seats.

Then we got in. "My first limo," I said. Inside there was a TV set and a telephone and a bar!

"First stop, the studio," Fritz said.

The limo whizzed along while my

parents and Duz and I looked out the windows and played with the TV.

At last it stopped in front of a big gate. A man in a uniform said, "Welcome to the studio, Mr. Khan."

Duz barked.

The gates opened. Duz barked again. He was acting like a big movie star already!

We drove past movie sets. First we went down a Wild West street. Then past a space station. Then a castle on a hill.

I saw people in weird costumes. A dress covered with cobwebs. A gorilla suit. And something that was green fuzz from head to toe. Ugh!

We got out of the limo and went into a

huge building. There were lights and wires and cameras and sets.

I stared and stared. I hoped I would see a real movie star.

Suddenly Duz was surrounded by four people. All I could see was his nose, poking to get out.

I knew two of the people. Duz's agent, Zero Fogg. And Mr. Swaggs, producer from Slambang Entertainment.

Mr. Swaggs and Zero patted Duz. They shook hands with my parents and me.

Zero said, "Welcome! Duz, I want you to meet your makeup person, Mr. Cosmos. And your acting coach, Ms. Muddlewolf."

Duz raised an ear.

Mr. Cosmos bent over him. "This dog will fluff well," he said. "And the camera will *love* his tail!"

Ms. Muddlewolf yelled, "Sit!"

Duz was already sitting.

"Good response time," she said.

"Come," Zero said.

We followed Zero and Mr. Swaggs down a long hall. There were huge photos of famous movie stars on the walls.

We went into a big room.

I saw a table full of weird-looking food. Ugly green leafy stuff, brown rice, sprouts, and some ooshy white glop. Was this California food?

Then I saw a second table. It was lower to the ground. *All* the food looked good on that one. Roast beef, baloney, and a big hamburger shaped like a star.

And cookies! Shaped like stars.

I walked over and reached for a cookie.

"Stop!" Zero said. "That's dog food! That table is for our star!"

"Kibble that looks like a cookie?" I said.

"We do everything right in Hollywood," Mr. Swaggs said.

Duz walked around his table. He sniffed. He licked his teeth. He looked at me.

"Yes, movie star!" I said. "It's all yours! Eat! Eat!"

Duz lunged for the baloney.

He gobbled away. He was one happy movie star. I laughed.

Then I stopped laughing. Something sharp was digging into my shoulder.

3

A cat was sitting on me! It was the biggest cat I had ever seen. And it looked mean and tough.

A tall, thin woman rushed into the room. She grabbed the cat.

"Empress Geca didn't hurt you, did she?" she asked.

"I guess not," I said. "What kind of name is Empress Geca?"

"Empress means that she's an important cat. But only my cat and I know what Geca means."

Weird secret, I thought. Was everything weird in Hollywood? First the food, now the cat's name.

"She's trained," the woman said. "She can do anything. She loves to pretend to attack. Want to see?"

"No thanks," I said quickly.

Mr. Swaggs said, "Shedds, meet Veronica Slye, Duz's PR person."

"I'm the one who will get Duz's name in the newspapers and his face on TV," Veronica said.

"And you'll spread the word about his new movie," Mr. Swaggs said.

He patted something that looked like a thick book. "The movie script," he said. *"Genghis Khan: The Challenge."*

"What is the challenge?" I asked.

Mr. Swaggs grinned. "Genghis will be up against the most fearsome, frightening creature ever seen on a movie screen! The SLIME-OOOOOZY!"

Duz looked up. Then he went on munching. He didn't much care who he'd be up against. But I did.

"Duz may look mean," I said, "but he's gentle. He can't fight a horrible creature like that! You need a...a...stunt dog!"

"Don't worry," said Mr. Swaggs. "This fearsome creature will be created with computers, sound effects, et cetera."

"Thank goodness the SLIME-OOOOOZY isn't *real*," my mother muttered.

"Duz has to report to the set tomorrow," Zero said.

Veronica sighed. "This dog needs *months* of training. Can he jump on command, make a bow, do tricks? Can he *act*? Can he show sadness? Or love? Watch! Geca, HUG!!"

Suddenly Geca's whiskers were brushing my face. She was hugging me. Yuck!

Duz raised an ear. He had a new look on his face. Not mean. Scared! Scared of Geca.

"*Un*hug me!" I yelled at Geca. "Your

claws are making little holes in my T-shirt."

Veronica took Geca and kissed her.

Zero laughed. "Ms. Muddlewolf will train Duz. This is an action picture. No hugs."

"Duz will be terrific," Mr. Swaggs said.

He bent over and put a rhinestone collar around Duz's neck. Geca glared at Duz.

"Time to take the star and his family to their new home," Mr. Swaggs said.

Duz bent over and grabbed another hunk of baloney.

Fritz came around with the limo.

Duz jumped in. He sniffed the leather seats again. And the carpet. Duz had had a big sniff day so far. The crowds. The food. The limo.

"Duz," I said, "when you're a star, I guess that Hollywood is just one big sniff-fest."

Duz wagged his tail. And then we were off!

4

We drove through neighborhoods with huge homes and big trees. At last we turned up a long, winding path. We stopped in front of a house that looked like it belonged to a...well...a movie star! Awesome!

There were acres and acres. With palm trees. And a swimming pool.

"This is *ours?*" my father said.

"Your home sweet home for a year," Fritz told us.

He handed us some keys. "One for each

of you. And here's a key to the pool house."

Then he turned to Duz. "I'll pick you up at five A.M. tomorrow."

"*That* early?" my mother asked.

"Yes," said Fritz. "Genghis has to go to makeup first."

"To Mr. Cosmos?" I said. "But how long could it take to make up a *dog*?"

"Long," Fritz said. "They shine his claws. Polish his teeth. Sometimes they spray on dirt or blood."

Fritz opened the trunk of the limo. "I almost forgot," he said. "I have something for the star."

Fritz pulled out three sacks.

"Your fan mail so far," he said to Duz. Duz grabbed a sack in his teeth and headed for the front door. Fritz and I carried the other two up to the house. Then he drove off.

Suddenly the door opened.

A man and a woman were standing there. All dressed up in stiff black-and-white uniforms. They bowed slightly.

The man said, "Welcome. I am Charles, Master Duz's butler."

The woman said, "I am Diana, Master Duz's maid."

My mother looked at my father. "I'm not believing this," she said.

There was more not to believe. The house had fifteen rooms. Thick carpets. Lots of mirrors. Furniture like in a palace. A fountain in the living room. And paintings of famous movie star dogs in gold frames in every room.

"Beautiful, just beautiful!" my mother gasped.

Duz sniffed out the place. He found a room we hadn't seen yet.

It was his own bedroom. It had paintings of Rin Tin Tin, Lassie, Benji, and Toto. And Duz. All the greats. And in the middle of the room was Duz's bed. It was shaped like a gigantic bone!

Duz leaped up on his bed. He barked and wagged his tail.

"Okay, movie star," I said. "Now let's open your fan mail."

I dragged a sack into the room. I stuck my hand inside.

"One of these envelopes is huge. I'll open it. Now, Duz, are you ready for your first fan letter?"

Duz raised an ear.

There was a piece of cardboard inside the big envelope. I pulled it out. There were words printed with big letters on it. I read them.

DEAR DUZ SHEDD

(ALIAS GENGHIS KHAN)

I'M COMING TO GET YOU

YOU BELONG TO ME

SIGNED

YOUR REAL OWNER

I grabbed Duz.

I wanted to hold on to him forever.

He started to whimper. He knew we were in trouble.

"We have to call the police," my father said. "Or the FBI!"

"Wait a minute!" I said. "*Real* owner? What does that mean? I'm Duz's real owner."

I looked at Duz. "You're mine," I said. "I found you. You found me. We found each other."

Duz wagged his tail.

"And you certainly tried to find his real owner," my mother said. "I mean..."

"You mean his *previous* owner," my father said. "His former owner, his once-upon-a-time owner, his no-longer owner."

"It's okay, Dad," I said. "I know what you're trying to say. Somebody else must have owned Duz before us. But I sure couldn't find whoever it was."

"Well, I've figured this out," my mother said. "Everybody knows that this stray dog is getting rich and famous. Now somebody wants Duz's money."

"So, do we call the FBI?" my father asked.

I shrugged.

My mother said, "What if this scares Zero Fogg and Mr. Swaggs and all the movie people? What if they don't want Duz to be Genghis anymore?"

My father frowned. "On the other hand, if we tell them, maybe they'll hire a body-guard for Duz. All the really important stars have bodyguards. Arnold and Mel and Clint."

"Let's not tell anybody," I said. "Not now, anyway. What if the letter is just a joke?"

I kept holding on to Duz. "I wish you could tell us what to do next," I said to him.

Duz raised an ear. Then he started to chew on the letter.

"You're tampering with evidence!" my father yelled. "The FBI *hates* that!"

Duz slunk back.

"Sorry I yelled, Duz," my father said.

"Duz just told us what to do," I said. "He bit the letter. He says we shouldn't be scared. He says we should take action.

We should try to find out who wrote this letter."

"Are you sure he was telling us that?" my mother asked.

"Well, it works for me," my father said.

"Okay, exactly what do we *do*?" my mother asked.

I turned to Duz. "Well?"

Duz stretched out on his bone-bed.

"What does that mean?" my father asked.

"It means he's through giving advice," I said. "Or he's tired."

I looked at the postmark on the envelope. It wasn't clear.

"I can't tell where this was mailed from," I said. "It could be California or..."

"Or where?" my mother asked.

"Back home," I said. "Think about it. I found Duz back home. That's where he was a stray. So this pretend real owner could live in our hometown."

"Or he could have followed us to California," my mother said.

"Maybe we can find out," I said. "I'll call Pamela and ask her to check around."

I dialed long distance. I know Pamela's number by heart.

She answered. "Hello. Pamela Brinkman speaking."

It was great to hear her voice!

"Pamela," I began. "I need your help. Duz got a terrible letter. Somebody is coming to get him. Somebody who says he's Duz's real owner."

"Bad, bad stuff," Pamela said. "I'll catch the next plane to California."

Pamela is rich. She can go wherever she wants. If her parents say yes.

"Thanks," I said. "But you can help

right where you are. See, maybe whoever wrote the letter is there...where I found Duz."

"Gotcha," Pamela said. "I'll get right on it. Bye."

Pamela hung up. I wanted to tell her I missed her. But she was in a hurry to help me. What a friend!

I patted Duz. "That takes care of the home front. But we still have to watch you every minute. Somebody might try and take you."

"But *who?*" my mother asked.

"Master Duz!" Charles the butler was standing in the doorway. He was carrying a gold tray. "Time for Master Duz's snack," he said.

Charles placed the tray on the floor.

Duz wagged his tail.

Charles started to leave.

Suddenly I wondered, maybe Charles wasn't a *real* butler! And what about Diana? Maybe they're here to grab Duz when they get a chance.

"Charles," I said. "Who did you and Diana work for before you came here?"

"The queen of England, the president of the United States. And various dogs," Charles said.

Charles bowed and left.

"Well," my mother said, "Charles seems okay."

I looked out the darkened window. Maybe so. But somebody out there was coming after my dog. And I was scared.

6

"Look at the newspapers!"

My mother and father rushed into Duz's room.

It was almost 5:00 in the morning. Duz and I were stretched out on his bone-bed eating breakfast on trays.

I picked up a newspaper. "I see these at the supermarket," I said "They give you news about aliens eating pizza in New Jersey."

"This is worse," my father said. "Look at these headlines!"

I looked.

WHO IS GENGHIS KHAN'S REAL OWNER? WILL HOLLYWOOD SHED THE SHEDDS? KAN KHAN'S KAREER BE OVER?

"Our secret!" I gasped. "Somebody leaked our secret."

"It has to be Charles and Diana," my mother said.

Just then the doorbell chimed. It played the Genghis theme song.

"Fritz is here," I said.

I opened the door.

Fritz looked grim. "Mr. Swaggs wants to see your folks and you," he said.

"Duz is coming too," I said. "I'm not letting him out of my sight! *Ever!!*"

My mother, father, Duz, and I piled into the limo.

This was supposed to be Duz's first day of work in Hollywood.

But I was terrified to go to the studio.

We went straight to Mr. Swaggs's office. He was pacing up and down the room.

"Major! This is a major problem!" he bellowed. Then he sat down at the head of a long table.

Zero Fogg was on his right.

Veronica Slye was on his left. Empress Geca was on her shoulder.

When Duz saw Geca, he turned around to leave.

"It's okay, Duz," I said.

Geca stared at Duz. Then she sort of hissed.

"Sit down, Shedds," Mr. Swaggs said.

We did. There wasn't any food this time. The table was covered with alien-pizza newspapers.

Mr. Swaggs cleared his throat. "There

seems to be a question about who really owns Duz."

Zero spoke up. "The Shedds own Duz. Any crackpot could *claim* to own him."

Mr. Swaggs rubbed his forehead. "True," he said. "But can you *prove* you own him? If somebody else claims him, our contract might be worthless."

"We have a license for him," I said. "And we gave him shots. And flea powder and a leash and a bowl and bones and love."

Duz put his head on my lap.

"Fred's right," Zero said. "Besides, the police think the letter could be a prank."

"I'm sorry," said Mr. Swaggs. "But we need to replace Duz with another dog now."

My parents gasped. Zero Fogg looked stunned.

"What?" said Veronica. "You can't hire another dog. You had a contest. You picked this dog as the winner. The public will hate you."

I stood up. "You better believe it," I said. "I'm going to tell those alien-pizza newspapers, and the TV programs and everybody in the world, how you're treating my dog!"

Zero stood up. "Look," he said. "The cameras are ready to roll. We've got a script, we've got sets, all we need is a mean-looking Genghis. And he's sitting right here."

Duz raised an ear.

Mr. Swaggs groaned. "Okay, okay, let's shoot this movie as fast as we can. But if the real owner shows up, that's it. Meeting's over."

I grabbed Duz. We walked out of the building with my parents.

A reporter was waiting. I could tell he was from one of those alien-pizza newspapers.

"Duz Shedd," I told him, "is ready to meet the SLIME-OOOOOZY!"

Duz growled.

7

Two weeks went by and nothing bad happened.

No more scary letters.

The newspapers quieted down.

But I didn't let Duz out of my sight.

Every day, he went to work.

Every day, I went with him.

I watched him being fitted for a suit, goggles, and boots.

I watched him pose for publicity photos. I watched him autograph the photos with his paw print. I watched while he was combed, brushed, massaged, and polished.

I watched him everywhere. At a movie premiere. In a fancy restaurant. Shopping on Rodeo Drive.

Then came the hard work. I watched Duz getting trained. I saw him sit, stand, walk, run, roll over, leap, growl, grunt, hang his head, droop his ears.

I saw him eat baloney.

That's what his acting coach, Ms. Muddlewolf, gave him for a reward.

Duz loves baloney.

He was having a great time.

I wasn't. I kept looking at strangers. Watching, watching.

Would one of them try to snatch Duz?

One day on the set, I heard footsteps behind me.

Slow, quiet steps.

Someone was sneaking up on me.

I whirled around.

I saw...Pamela!!

She hugged me. Then she ran and hugged Duz. His goggles fell off.

Then he licked Pamela's nose. He remembered her.

"Surprise!" she said. "I came to help you. I called your house from the airport. Your folks said you were here."

Pamela looked around. "I *love* this place. Ah, great eats. Can I have some baloney?" Pamela talked while she ate.

"I checked everything back home," she said "No leads at all. If there was a real owner in town, he's gone now. So I came here. I'm staying two weeks."

"Great," I said. "You'll like my house. You can have your choice of Rooms Number Three, Eight, Ten, or Eleven."

Pamela picked Number Eleven.

Then she grabbed what she thought was a cookie and stuffed it in her mouth.

Should I tell my best friend that she had just eaten a doggie treat?

8

Pamela went to the studio with Duz and me every day. We saw Duz learn to look sad and mad and happy. We saw him learn how to scrunch his nose and look amazed.

One day Ms. Muddlewolf said, "Tomorrow is it. We're shooting the first scene of the movie."

"What will Duz have to do in it?" Pamela asked.

"He walks in the woods," Ms. Muddlewolf said. "Suddenly he looks up and sees the SLIME-OOOOOZY's claw. Then he runs and hides behind some trees."

"Why doesn't he just attack?" Pamela asked.

"He has to *plan* his attack," Ms. Muddlewolf said.

"Duz knows how to walk and run," I said. "But how do you get him to look up and pretend to see a claw?"

"I hold up a big piece of baloney," Ms. Muddlewolf said. "That's what Duz will be looking at. It won't be in the movie, of course. The claw will."

"Duz will do great," Pamela said. "I knew him even before he was a star."

The next day Fritz drove my parents, me, Pamela, and Duz to some woods. He stopped in a clearing.

People were rushing around. There were lights and cameras. And trailers. And long tables and lots of chairs. It was like a little village in the woods.

I saw Mr. Swaggs, Zero Fogg, and Veronica Slye sitting together.

Veronica's cat was on her shoulder.

Duz shrunk back.

Ms. Muddlewolf came running from the woods to greet us.

"And here's our star," she said. She started to lead Duz away.

"Wait!" I said. "I go everywhere with him."

"He needs to go into makeup and costume," Ms. Muddlewolf said. "He'll be just fine."

Duz trotted along beside her happily. He was a movie star, ready to act.

They went into a trailer that had a big star on the door. Duz had his own trailer!

"Well, this is it," my mother said. "I'm the mother of a star."

"That makes you the brother," Pamela giggled.

I laughed. I felt so excited!

My parents and Pamela and I sat down next to Zero Fogg.

He said, "My client loves baloney. All will be well."

We waited a long time. At last somebody called, "Quiet, lights, camera, action," or something like that.

Suddenly, there was Duz. In a Genghis costume. Black leather. Blue satin. Goggles. Boots. Wow! Even *I* felt a little scared of him!

Now Duz was supposed to walk.

"In those boots?" my father gasped.

"His boots are fake," I whispered. "No bottoms."

Duz started to walk in the woods. So

far, so good. Duz knew how to walk.

Then I saw somebody sitting in a tree. It was Ms. Muddlewolf. She was holding a big hunk of baloney.

Duz looked up.

He kept looking.

I had never seen that look on his face before. Strange and strong.

Ms. Muddlewolf must be a genius to get him to look that way.

So far so good. Then Duz ran and hid behind some trees.

Duz was doing everything he was supposed to do!

"Bravo!" Zero said. "Great job. Duz is a natural."

"That's it?" I asked.

"For now," Zero said. "In the next scene, Duz attacks! Now let's go pat our star."

We all rushed toward the woods.

Ms. Muddlewolf was climbing down from the tree. She was grinning.

"Duz *became* Genghis!" she said. "Did you see that? A dog star is born."

Mr. Swaggs waved to us. A very happy wave. My mother and father were jumping up and down.

"Duz *did* it," my mother said.

"I have a giant hunk of baloney for our star," Ms. Muddlewolf said. "Where *is* our star?"

Zero chuckled. "Maybe he's waiting for a signal to come out of the woods."

Ms. Muddlewolf held up the baloney. "I'm sure he can smell this," she said.

"Duz!" I called.

Duz didn't come.

"Maybe that name doesn't work anymore," Pamela said. "Genghis!" she called.

Duz didn't come.

I was getting a bad feeling.

I felt clammy and shivery.

I had guarded Duz, I had watched over him, and now...

What I had been afraid of...had it happened?

Pamela and I ran into the woods. My parents ran after us. Ms. Muddlewolf ran after them. Zero and Mr. Swaggs ran after her.

We all yelled, "DUZ! DUZ!"

We ran and ran.

We yelled and yelled.

But my Duz, my wonderful dog, was gone.

"Everybody look for him!" Mr. Swaggs commanded. *"Everybody!"*

People spread out in all directions.

Pamela said, "I want to check out that tree. The one Duz hid behind."

Pamela and I walked around and around the tree. We looked up and down.

"Hey, I see something," Pamela said. "A piece of shiny blue cloth."

Pamela grabbed it from a branch.

"It's from Duz's costume!" I said.

"It's full of little holes," Pamela said. She handed it to me.

"Duz must have snagged it on the branch," I said.

"I guess it's not really a clue," Pamela said. "We know Duz was here anyway."

I put the piece of cloth in my pocket. I wanted to keep it close to me. It belonged to Duz.

"Let's look for more pieces," I said. "Maybe Duz left a trail."

We looked for more pieces. We didn't find any. Not one.

Nobody else had any luck either. Nobody found clues. Nobody found Duz.

At last Mr. Swaggs said, "I'm afraid that Duz has been kidnapped. We'll have to tell the police. But what do I tell the newspapers?"

"That's Veronica's job," Zero said. "Where is she?"

"Her cat ran off and she ran after her," Mr. Swaggs said. "There they are now."

"That's one animal I'd like to lose," Zero said. "I wish someone would kidnap that little monster."

"Forget her," I said. "My dog is gone. And I've got to go to the police right now."

"They'll find Duz," Pamela said.

But I kept thinking, *What if they can't?*

Two days passed. No sign of Duz.

We all cried. Mom, Dad, Pamela, me.

Charles and Diana kept serving us tea and asking if they could help.

At night I slept in the bone-bed. It smelled of Duz. I hoped he wasn't hurt. I hoped he was *alive*!

The newspapers had terrible new headlines.

DOG-GONE!!
GENGHIS KHAN'T BE FOUND!
DUZ DUZN'T APPEAR!
SHEDDS SHED TEARS

The police kept working on the case. They ran tests on the letter.

Nothing. Except Duz's teeth marks.

Fritz kept bringing more fan mail. We kept looking for a letter from the kidnapper. Nothing. Just cheer-up notes.

On the third day Mr. Swaggs phoned me. He said that the show must go on. That we had to be practical.

I said, "You mean you're dumping Duz."

He said, "Dump? We can't *find* him."

Pamela grabbed the phone. "Fred will find Duz," she promised. And she hung up.

I groaned. "How can I do that?"

"We've got to think about what was going on when Duz disappeared."

"Okay", I said. "The kidnapper had to be around when the scene was shot."

"But," said Pamela, "a lot of people

were there. And the kidnapper was probably hiding in the woods anyway."

"Duz's costume wasn't found," I said. "Wouldn't somebody notice a dog in that costume?"

"Maybe the kidnapper took it off and carried it away in a bag," Pamela said.

"Well, the police looked at the movie film over and over for clues. All they saw was Duz."

"Hey, maybe *we* saw something that means something," Pamela said.

"Oh?"

"And maybe *you* know something you don't think you know."

"Oh?" I said again.

"Yeah," Pamela made a face. "If only you knew what it was."

The next day Mr. Swaggs phoned again.

"No Duz?" he said.

"No Duz," I said.

"Then we need to have a meeting *now*."

Fritz drove my parents, Pamela, and me to the studio. I missed Duz sniffing the limo leather.

Mr. Swaggs, Zero Fogg, and Veronica Slye were waiting for us. Veronica's cat was walking up and down the table. Veronica said, "Geca, stop!"

Geca stopped. Then she purred. It sounded like a lion's roar.

My father muttered, "Crazy cat, crazy name."

Mr. Swaggs said, "Unfortunately, Duz hasn't been found. We need to replace him with another dog."

"No!" said Veronica.

I smiled. At least somebody was on my side.

"It's not the right thing to do," she

said. "You have scenes that Duz isn't in. You could shoot those next."

"But what happens after I do them and Duz still isn't found?" said Mr. Swaggs.

"Well, then you'll get another animal actor," Veronica said. "I have lots of friends in the animal world. Look how well-trained Empress Geca is."

"Can you train dogs?" I asked.

"One thing at a time," Veronica said.

"Very well," said Mr. Swaggs. "We'll shoot the scenes that Duz isn't in. Then we'll meet here on Friday. Duz had better show up by then."

He looked at me. "You have a real friend in Veronica."

We went home. That night I dreamed about Veronica. And Geca. The name still sounded weird, even in my dream.

11

The police were getting nowhere. Charles and Diana were serving us more and more tea. Fritz was bringing more and more fan mail.

Pamela said she would stay in Hollywood until Duz was found.

"That could be forever," I said.

"You'll find Duz," she said. "You *will!*"

Was Pamela right?

Somewhere in my head bits of information were adding up. I had this itchy feeling that I had enough clues to find Duz.

But time was almost up. It was Thursday night. Tomorrow was the meeting at the studio. I knew that Mr. Swaggs would dump Duz from the movie.

I took the piece of blue cloth out of my pocket. Poor Duz.

I stared at the cloth. I felt it.

Could the cloth mean something?

Then I picked up the script for *Genghis Khan: The Challenge.*

I kept looking at the title.

Genghis. That name—it *meant* something.

I said it over and over.

Genghis, Genghis, Genghis.

Then I thought about the cloth *and* the name.

I got very excited!

I said to Pamela, "Quick, we need to go to the police."

12

Early Friday morning Fritz drove us to the studio.

"This is it!" I said to Pamela.

My parents looked nervous. The four of us got out of the limo.

Fritz said, "You can count on me."

Inside the studio, Mr. Swaggs, Zero Fogg, and Veronica Slye were sitting in their usual places. Empress Geca was walking up and down the table.

Veronica said, "Geca, stop!" Geca stopped. Veronica said, "Geca, jump!" Geca jumped onto Veronica's shoulder.

"Greetings, Shedds and Pamela," Mr. Swaggs said. "Please sit down."

Mr. Swaggs cleared his throat. "Unfortunately," he said, "Duz hasn't come back. We've finished shooting the scenes in which Genghis doesn't appear. We need a new Genghis *now.*"

"And I have the answer," Veronica said. "I know a trained animal who can step right into the part. Someone I've rehearsed."

Zero Fogg leaned forward. "Oh?" he said. "Who?"

"Jump!" Veronica said.

Empress Geca leaped off her shoulder onto the table.

Veronica cried, "Meet Genghis Cat!"

"Wh-a-a-a-t?" Mr. Swaggs looked stupefied. "You want a movie called *Genghis* CAT: *The Challenge?*"

"Why not?" said Veronica. "She's big,

she's ugly, she can jump, she can attack. She was *born* to be Genghis!"

Mr. Swaggs rocked back and forth. "Oh please, please tell me I'm dreaming. Genghis *Cat*? Life is cruel."

Veronica picked up her cat. "Sweetie, let's tell them what the name Geca stands for. *Ge* as in Genghis, *ca* as in cat."

Pamela nudged me. "You were right."

I stood up. "Thanks for the offer of your cat, Veronica. But my parents and Pamela and I found someone who will be a perfect Genghis." I snapped my fingers.

Fritz walked in with a dog.

Mr. Swaggs leaped up. "I'm saved! That dog looks just like Genghis Khan! Exactly! Where did you find him?"

"Tell him, Veronica," I said.

Veronica sneered. "I don't know what you're talking about."

Two police officers stepped into the room.

"What's going on here?" Mr. Swaggs shouted.

"I'll tell you what," I said. I rushed over to the dog and put my arm around him. "This dog, I'm happy to say, is...my DUZ!! Veronica Slye kidnapped him!"

Duz wagged his tail wildly. He licked my face like it was made of baloney.

I went on. "After you left your house this morning, Veronica, the police went in. They found Duz."

Zero Fogg scratched his head. "I thought Duz was kidnapped by someone who claimed to be his real owner."

My mother spoke up. "Veronica made up that real-owner business. She didn't want us to suspect her. She wrote that letter to scare us so we'd get Duz out of town. She must have told the newspapers too. To make us more scared."

Pamela nodded. "She wanted that job for her cat from the very beginning."

"But the letter didn't work. Duz kept his job," I said.

Mr. Swaggs looked confused. "When I saw the newspapers and wanted to replace Duz, why did Veronica talk me out of it?"

"Simple," I said. "She sure didn't want another *dog*. She was stalling. She decided to kidnap Duz after you'd shot some of the movie. With Duz gone, she hoped you'd become desperate. Then you'd accept her cat as Genghis."

I walked up to Veronica. "You pretended

to be my friend," I said. "But it was all a scheme to make your cat a movie star."

Veronica gave me a mean look.

I gave her a mean look back. "You kidnapped Duz when you went into the woods after your cat," I said.

Veronica gave me a meaner look.

I went on. "You must have whispered a command to Geca to run into the woods. It gave you an excuse to run after her and kidnap Duz. You put Duz in your car and drove home. Then you and Geca came back."

"You little wise guy!" Veronica said.

"You pretended that Geca was running away on her own," I said. "But if that was so, all you had to do was yell, *Geca, stop!* Geca would have obeyed. But you didn't. You ran after her. You trapped yourself by having a trained cat."

My father said, "My son figured that out all by himself!"

Pamela spoke up. "There's even more. We found a piece of Duz's costume on the tree. It had small holes in it."

"Just like my T-shirt got when Geca hugged me," I said. "When I remembered that, I knew that Geca was right there when Duz was kidnapped."

Veronica's face turned bright red. She shouted, "All the good roles go to dogs! Down with dogs! Cats are clean, cats are neat, cats are smart."

Veronica's face got redder. "Dogs are flea bait. And they slobber and whine. But they get to be stars. Where are all the jobs for cats? My poor Geca. Every day, sipping her milk, dreaming of fame..."

Suddenly Veronica waved her arms. "Geca," she screamed. "Att—"

The word was *attack*. I knew it. But before she could finish, I heard a terrible growl.

"GRRRRRRRRRRRRRRRRRRRrrrr!!!!"

Duz leaped on the table, ready to fight. Geca backed off.

Mr. Swaggs danced around the room. "My Genghis, my Genghis, he's truly back!!"

The police started to lead Veronica away.

Empress Geca padded behind them.

Veronica called to me. "I was going to let Duz go. Right after Geca did her first scene. I knew the studio wouldn't even *want* Duz after they saw my Geca. She doesn't need baloney. How about that!!"

13

I'm sitting at my swimming pool with my Duz.

Blue skies. Sunshine. My toes in the warm water.

I'm happy. Everybody I know is happy.

Except Veronica. She was sentenced to work at a dog shelter for six months.

Maybe she'll learn to love dogs.

Then again, maybe not.

Duz sleeps alone in his bone-bed now.

He's a bigger star than ever.

He gets so many sacks of mail that I

gave up carrying them. Charles and Diana do it, one sack at a time.

Duz is halfway through the movie.

People say that he might even win an Academy Award for his acting.

He now owns five rhinestone collars. And a diamond one for dress-up.

That's the way they do things in Hollywood.

And Duz has another contract. To write a book. About how it felt to be kidnapped by the cat lady.

He's starting the book right after he finishes his *Shape Up with Duz* exercise video.

As I said, that's the way they do things in Hollywood.

Don't miss the next Genghis Khan book!

I opened the newspaper.

I started reading.

> Our next Academy Award winner?
> I predict that Duz Shedd, world-
> famous for his canine role in
> *Genghis Khan: The Challenge*,
> will win next year's Academy
> Award as best actor. Move over,
> Mel and Clint. Make room for the
> biggest star of them all—Duz
> Shedd.
>   Duz, make room for your
> Oscar!

I couldn't believe it. Duz had made only one movie and he was already a Hollywood great.

From *Genghis Khan: The Envelope Please!*
by Marjorie Weinman Sharmat

Don't miss the *first* Genghis Khan book!

Aaaah!!!

I was playing ball with a few kids. The ball went into the woods.

We started to look for it.

Suddenly we saw it. It was in the mouth of the meanest-looking dog I had ever seen.

Huge. Big teeth. Big claws. Glaring eyes. SCARY!

"Aaaah!!" yelled one of the kids.

Everyone fled.

Except me. It was my ball.

From *The Great Genghis Khan Look-Alike Contest* by Marjorie Weinman Sharmat

MARJORIE WEINMAN SHARMAT is best known for creating super-sleuth Nate the Great. Her books have been translated into fourteen languages and have won numerous awards. She insists that Duz is not based on her dog, Dudley—who, she says, is "definitely cute" and has never starred in a movie.

Ms. Sharmat lives with her husband, Mitchell. They have two sons—Craig and Andrew—and a grandson, Nathan.